For Esie

Aladdin Paperbacks
An imprint of Simon & Schuster
Children's Publishing Division
1230 Avenue of the Americas
New York, New York 10020

Copyright © 1986 by Paul Galdone

Printed in Hong Kong

15   14   13   12   11   10   9   8

Library of Congress Cataloging-in-Publication Data
Galdone, Paul
Over in the meadow.
Summary: An old nursery poem introduces animals and
their young and the numbers one through ten.
1. Nursery rhymes.   2. Children's poetry.
[1. Nursery rhymes.   2. Animals—Poetry.   3. Counting]
I. Title.
PZ8.3.G12180v   1986   398'8   85-24664
ISBN 0-671-67837-X

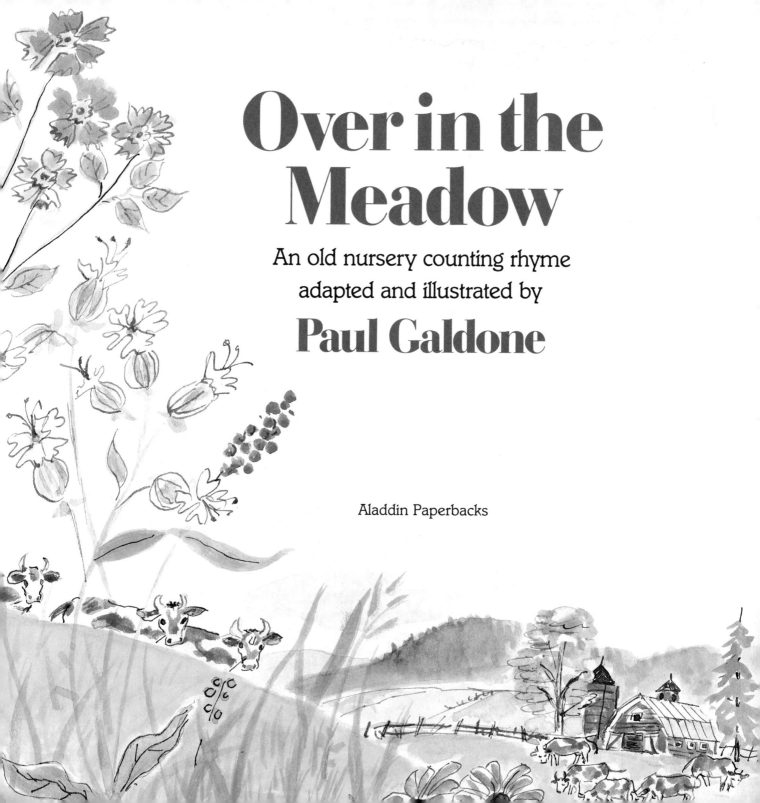

Over in the Meadow

An old nursery counting rhyme
adapted and illustrated by

Paul Galdone

Aladdin Paperbacks

Over in the meadow
in the sand in the sun
Lived an old mother turtle
and her little turtle

one

Hide, said the mother.
I hide, said the one.
So she hid all day
in the sand in the sun.

Over in the meadow
in a pond so blue
Lived a green mother frog
and her little froggies

two

Jump, said the mother.
We jump, said the two.
So they jumped all day
in a pond so blue.

Over in the meadow
near a fallen tree
Lived a brown mother beaver
and her little beavers

three

Gnaw, said the mother.
We gnaw, said the three.
So they gnawed all day
near the fallen tree.

Over in the meadow
by the red barn door
Lived a gray mother mouse
and her little mice four

Squeak, said the mother.
We squeak, said the four.
So they squeaked all day
by the red barn door.

Over in the meadow
where the wildflowers thrive
Lived a busy mother bee
and her little bees

five

Buzz, said the mother.
We buzz, said the five.
So they buzzed all day
where the wildflowers thrive.

Over in the meadow
   in a nest built of sticks
Lived a noisy mother crow
   and her little crows

six

Caw, said the mother.
We caw, said the six.
So they cawed all day
in a nest built of sticks.

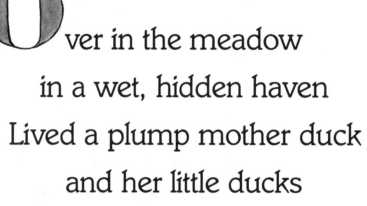

Over in the meadow
in a wet, hidden haven
Lived a plump mother duck
and her little ducks

seven

Quack, said the mother.
We quack, said the seven.
So they quacked all day
in a wet, hidden haven.

Over in the meadow
by the barnyard gate
Lived a pink mother pig
and her little piglets

eight

Oink, said the mother.
We oink, said the eight.
So they oinked all day
by the barnyard gate.

Over in the meadow
in the stream by the pine
Lived a quick mother fish
and her little fishes

nine

Swim, said the mother.
We swim, said the nine.
So they swam all day
in the stream by the pine.

Over in the meadow
in a soft, warm den
Lived a red mother fox
and her little foxes

ten

Sleep, said the mother.
We sleep, said the ten.
So they slept all night
in the soft, warm den.

Goodnight